Grey Rabbit and the Wandering Hedgehog

Alison Uttley

pictures by Margaret Tempest

Collins

William Collins Sons & Co Ltd
London · Glasgow · Sydney · Auckland
Toronto · Johannesburg

First published 1948
© text The Alison Uttley Literary Property Trust 1988
© illustrations The Estate of Margaret Tempest 1988
© this arrangement William Collins Sons & Co Ltd 1988
Cover decoration by Fiona Owen
Decorated capital by Mary Cooper
Alison Uttley's original story has been abridged for this book.
Uttley, Alison
Grey Rabbit and the Wandering Hedgehog. —
Rev. ed. — (Little Grey Rabbit books)
I. Title   II. Tempest, Margaret
III. Series
823'.912 [J] PZ7

ISBN 0-00-194264-6

Typeset by Columns of Reading
Made and Printed in Great Britain by
William Collins Sons and Co Ltd, Glasgow

FOREWORD

Of course you must understand that Grey Rabbit's home had no electric light or gas, and even the candles were made from pith of rushes dipped in wax from the wild bees' nests, which Squirrel found. Water there was in plenty, but it did not come from a tap. It flowed from a spring outside, which rose up from the ground and went to a brook. Grey Rabbit cooked on a fire, but it was a wood fire, there was no coal in that part of the country. Tea did not come from India, but from a little herb known very well to country people, who once dried it and used it in their cottage homes. Bread was baked from wheat ears, ground fine, and Hare and Grey Rabbit gleaned in the cornfields to get the wheat.

The doormats were plaited rushes, like country-made mats, and cushions were stuffed with wool gathered from the hedges where sheep pushed through the thorns. As for the looking-glass, Grey Rabbit found the glass, dropped from a lady's handbag, and Mole made a frame for it. Usually the animals gazed at themselves in the still pools as so many country children have done. The country ways of Grey Rabbit were the country ways known to the author.

ne day when Grey Rabbit was walking in the lane, she saw a tiny spire of blue smoke twisting from the hedge. She sniffed at the smell of the smoke and it was very sweet, like cherry-wood. Then another smell came to her. It was a savoury stew. She took a step, and listened. Somebody was busy; she could hear the rattle of sticks and the chink of a tin can.

Then a voice began to sing:

"I haven't got a coat, and I haven't got a
shoe,
I haven't got a penny, and I haven't got a
sou.
I don't care a jot, I've got my cooking-pot,
And the whole wide world is mine to wander
through."

There sat a ragged little Hedgehog, dirty and dusty. He stirred a round tin pan over a fire. He danced a step and waved his wooden spoon, and Grey Rabbit thought he hadn't seen her. She was very surprised when he called out:

"Grey Rabbit, Grey Rabbit, I see you hiding there. Come out."

Shyly she stepped from her shelter and stood before him.

"Well, Grey Rabbit, you don't know me, do you?"

"No," she faltered. "I've not seen you before."

"I am a wanderer. I travel the world. You stay at home, but I go up and down the country."

"Oh! You must be Brush, the Wandering Hedgehog," said Grey Rabbit.

"True! I haven't a roof over my head, Grey Rabbit. In the winter I sleep under yonder oak tree, but the rest of the year I enjoy myself, seeing life."

"You seem very happy out here," said Grey Rabbit, looking at his ancient hat with its blue feather.

"Will you taste my good broth, Grey Rabbit?" asked the ragged Hedgehog.

He ladled a few spoonfuls into a little wooden bowl, then he took another bowl and filled it for himself.

"Sit here, Grey Rabbit." He patted a tuft of moss and Grey Rabbit smoothed her blue apron and seated herself opposite to him. She sipped the broth and it was indeed delicious.

"Grey Rabbit," said the Hedgehog, "will you do me a favour?"

"Oh yes," said Grey Rabbit, quickly.

"I wondered if you have a cast-off, done-with, thrown-away coat of Mister Hare's that I could have? It's cold in the winter, wandering the world, before I get to my little house in the oak tree."

"There's a red coat of Hare's," said Grey Rabbit. "It will be rather large, I fear, but I could alter it to fit you."

"Thank you, Grey Rabbit. In return, I would like to give you a present."

He cut a piece of an elder stem and made a little whistle out of it. When Grey Rabbit put it to her lips and blew hard, a lovely mellow note came from it

So Grey Rabbit sat by the fire with the Wandering Hedgehog, while he told her tales. Once, she leaned over and put a branch on the flames, and watched the sparks fly. She blacked her face and she tore her apron, but she didn't care.

At last she remembered the family at home and she said good-bye.

Hare was swinging on the gate and Squirrel was sitting in the apple tree.

"There you are at last, Grey Rabbit," said Hare. "We are as hungry as hunters. Where have you been all this time?"

"Oh, I've been talking to Brush the Wandering Hedgehog," she cried.

"That beggarly old Hedgehog!" cried Hare. "Really Grey Rabbit."

"He was very nice." Grey Rabbit was indignant. "He gave me an elder whistle."

"Go on," said Hare. "I can see by your eyes there's something else."

"Yes," said Grey Rabbit. "He hasn't a coat and he asked if we could give him one."

"Whose coat?" asked Hare.

"Your coat, Hare," said Grey Rabbit.

"My coat!" Hare leaped so high in surprise that his head touched the apple tree and knocked off some of the blossom.

"Grey Rabbit, what did you say?"

"I told him he could have your coat."

"Over my dead body," said Hare.

"Nobody else has a coat," said Grey Rabbit. "Squirrel hasn't one, and I have only a cloak. He could have that."

"He can't have your blue cloak, Grey Rabbit," said Squirrel. "I wear it when it's cold. We all wear it."

"I have two coats," said Hare, a blue one for weekdays and a red one for Sundays. I shan't give either to any old Wandering Hedgehog."

"I'm hungry," said Squirrel. "I suppose you had dinner with that Hedgehog."

"Well, I did," confessed Grey Rabbit.

"You did? Oh, Grey Rabbit! You will become a raggle-taggle gipsy if you go on like this. Look at your apron. You've torn it. Look at your face. There's a black mark across it."

"I tore my apron on a briar bush, and I smudged my face helping Brush to stir his fire," whispered Grey Rabbit.

They all went indoors where the fire was low
and the potatoes were roasting in the embers.
Soon Grey Rabbit had a nice meal ready of
potatoes in their jackets with butter and salt
and mugs of milk.

When she looked out of the window she
could see the thin spire of smoke coming
from the hedge far away. She thought of the
Wandering Hedgehog sitting there all alone.
She did want to give him a coat.

Hare ran over the field and peered through the bushes at the Wandering Hedgehog. Brush began to sing:

"I haven't got a coat, and I haven't got a shoe,
I haven't got a penny, and I haven't got a sou.
I don't care a jot, I've got my cooking-pot,
And the whole wide world is mine to wander through."

Hare never moved.

"Thank you for the coat, Hare," called the Hedgehog. "It will suit me nicely."

"Eh?" exclaimed Hare. "You can't have my coat."

"Well anybody's coat will do," answered the Hedgehog.

Hare came closer. He sniffed the fire and he sniffed the Hedgehog's baccy.

"Like a puff?" said the Hedgehog.

The Hedgehog held out the dirty old pipe in his sooty hand. Hare wiped it on his handkerchief, and then he took a puff.

It was delicious! He took another. It was glorious! Then Hare noticed something very strange. As the smoke curled upward, it formed lovely shapes of trees and animals and hills.

"See anything?" asked the Hedgehog.

"Lots of things!" cried Hare excitedly.

"Them's my wanderings. They get into my baccy and comes out in smoke. Would you like a pipe for yourself, Hare?"

The Hedgehog cut a slip of elder wood. He hollowed it and made a pipe with an acorn cup for a bowl.

"Now what about a cup of tea, Mister Hare?"

"I don't mind if I do," said Hare.

Hedgehog poured steaming tea into two wooden bowls. "Like it?" he asked.

"I should think I do."

"Now about this coat," Hedgehog went on. "I don't want to rob you, Hare, but if you can get me a coat for the hard weather, well, I shall say, 'Thank ye'."

That seemed fair enough to Hare and he went home to talk it over with Grey Rabbit and Squirrel.

"The Wandering Hedgehog isn't such a bad fellow," he began.

"Oh," said Squirrel. "How do you know?"

"I just met him, and I had a hobnob with him," said Hare.

"Hare! You've been smoking. I can smell baccy on your clothes," said Squirrel.

"Well, yes," confessed Hare, "and he gave me a pipe for myself."

"And you've got a smudge on your cheek," said Squirrel.

"I say," said Hare. "Can we get a coat for that Hedgehog? He hasn't one, and when the frost comes he will feel cold."

"That dirty old ragamuffin!" cried Squirrel.

"He's not so dirty, Squirrel," said Hare.

Now, later on, Squirrel stepped daintily down the lane, swinging on the bushes and running along the branches.

She peered from a larch tree at the Hedgehog frying something on a toasting fork made from a twiggy branch.

She leaned forward and fell nearly on top of the Hedgehog.

"Good evening, Miss Squirrel," said he. "I seed you a-peeping at me."

"What are you doing?" asked Squirrel.

"It's a parasol mushroom I'm toasting for supper," replied the Hedgehog.

"Will you have a bite with me?"

"Yes, please," said Squirrel.

The Hedgehog was dirty, but his face was pleasant, and he had a merry smile. He poured out a bowl of nettle broth, and Squirrel sipped it with a wooden spoon. Then he gave her a toasted mushroom, black and juicy. It was very tasty, and Squirrel even licked her paws at the end.

Then the Hedgehog pulled up a flowering
rush. He peeled it, and twisted it into a
bracelet and held it out to Squirrel. She
slipped it on, and smiled at him.
Hedgehog talked of this and that, speaking
of his adventures, and Squirrel listened,
wide-eyed.

"About this coat, Miss Squirrel. If you could
see your way to getting a coat for me,
I should be much obliged," said he.

"Certainly," said Squirrel. "I will see if I can persuade Grey Rabbit and Hare to find you a coat."

She went off home and told her tale.

"So you've been to see that dirty old ragamuffin," teased Hare.

"You've got a smudge on your face, Squirrel," said Grey Rabbit.

"Really we must get a coat for that poor animal," said Squirrel. "There you sit, and nobody bothers to get a coat for him."

"So at last we are all agreed" laughed Grey Rabbit. She went to the chest of drawers and brought out some pieces of cloth, green and blue and red.

"Those wouldn't make a coat for a bumble-bee," said Hare. "I'll go and ask everyone for scraps, Grey Rabbit."

The next day when Milkman Hedgehog came to the door, Hare asked him.

"There's a relation of yours down the lane without a coat to his back. What are you going to do about it?"

"Him? That Wandering Hedgehog?" Old Hedgehog scratched his head. "You go and talk it over with my Missus, she'll maybe find you a bit of something."

Hare visited Mrs Hedgehog, and explained what he wanted.

"I'll give you a red spotted handkerchief," said she. "It will help. And here's a bit of an old blue smock of Fuzzypeg's."

Hare next went to see Moldy Warp in his house in the field.

"That Wandering Hedgehog?" cried Moldy Warp, shaking his head. "I know him. I'll give him a piece of black velvet, if that's any use."

Then Hare went to Water Rat's house. Water Rat was rowing his little boat when Hare found him.

"Something to make a coat for the Wandering Hedgehog?" asked Water Rat. "Here's a boat cushion, made of strong red cloth." He tossed a cushion ashore, and Hare caught it.

"Thank you Water Rat. This will suit the Hedgehog," and he ran home with it.

Then he went to see Wise Owl. Wise Owl muttered and grumbled when Hare rang his bell. "Be off! Be off!" he cried, and he threw a book at Hare.

Hare hurried back to Grey Rabbit. "We can't sew this," he said.

Grey Rabbit turned the pages. "'The Cutter and Tailor. How to make a coat out of bits and pieces'," she read. "This will be a great help. It's got a picture of a patchwork coat."

So Hare went to all the other houses to find some more pieces. He brought home such a collection of scraps and oddments, of silk and wool, of calico and linen, of leaves and moss, that Grey Rabbit threw up her paws when she saw them all.

"It's lucky we've Wise Owl's book to tell us how to make it," said she.

They sat round the table, with all the scraps spread out and planned the coat.

Grey Rabbit stitched them together, as Squirrel and Hare sorted them into shapes and colours. It was a fine patchwork, with golden yellow, and brown and orange, with blue and scarlet and crimson and black velvet.

Grey Rabbit used all the coloured cottons in her workbasket. She sewed on acorn buttons, and Squirrel embroidered the edge of the coat with feather-stitching.

"It's most beautiful," she cried, when at last Grey Rabbit held it up for all to see.

"It's like the rainbow," said Hare.

"It's like a garden full of flowers," said Squirrel.

"Let's take it to him now," cried Hare, leaping up.

Out they went in the moonlight, dancing with joy down the lane. There was the little fire burning, and by its side sat Brush, the Wandering Hedgehog. Although they walked very softly, he heard them coming.

"Hello Squirrel, and Hare and little Grey Rabbit. Have you brought it?"

"Yes, Brush. It's nicer than my old red coat," said Hare. "You are lucky this time."

"A coat of twenty colours," added Squirrel.

They held up the coat in the firelight and the old Hedgehog took his pipe from his mouth and stared.

"Never, never did I see a coat like this, not in all my born days," said he. "Nay, I'm wrong. Only once did I see one, and that was worn by the Emperor of China, but not as good as this."

He slipped his arms through the sleeves and buttoned the acorns down the front. He held up the sides and danced, while the three friends looked on.

Then he dived into the hedgerow and pulled out a little brown basket.

"Here's something for you in exchange. Don't open it till you get home. I shall be off on my travels tonight. I was just waiting for this coat, which I knowed was coming, and the new moon, and I knowed that was coming too. Now I shall be off."

The Wandering Hedgehog was already stamping out the fire. He gathered up his bundle, then away he turned down the lane, his hat on his head and his pipe in his mouth.

"Good-bye and good luck," they called.

They stared after him. They could hear his voice in the distance, singing his old song, with a slight difference:

"I've got a fine coat, and I haven't got a shoe,
I haven't got a penny, and I haven't got a sou.
I don't care a jot, I've got my cooking pot,
And the whole wide world is mine to wander through."

"What's in the basket?" asked Hare, trying to peep through the lid.

"Wait till we get home," warned Grey Rabbit.

So away they ran, leaping back to their house. They stood around while Hare took the wooden pin from the basket and lifted the lid. Inside lay a little brown Nightingale. She sang a sweet trilling song and then she flew out.

"She may make her nest in our garden," said Grey Rabbit.

The Nightingale sang again, as if to agree that it was just the place she wanted.

She built her nest with the help of her little
brown husband in the apple tree and there
she sat on her eggs. Every night Mr
Nightingale sang, and every day as well. It
was better even than having a musical box,
Grey Rabbit thought.

Far away the Wandering Hedgehog
roamed the lanes. He carried his coloured
coat in his pack, to keep it clean,
ready for the cold weather.